UM LAND

SILAS' STORY WITH PAUL'S ART

BOOK DESIGN BY
PAUL VIRLAN

PRINTED IN PRC BY
UM LAND PRESS

WWW.MYUMLAND.COM

ISBN: 13:978-0-692-13801-4 (HARDCOVER)

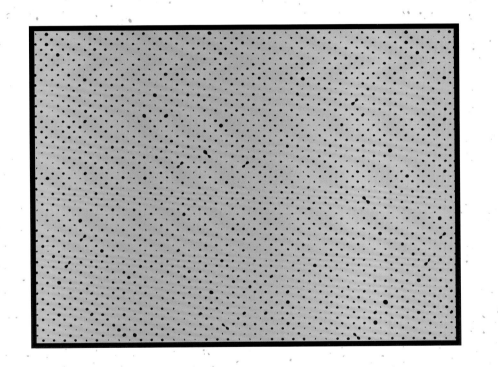

MY NAME IS SILAS!

I HAVE 9 MEMBERS IN MY FAMILY;

ONE IS SASSY, ONE IS STINKY,

ONE ONLY HAS ONE EYE,

ONE HAS GREEN HAIR,

ONE POPS **PIMPLES** AND CUTS WARTS FOR WORK,

ONE IS A FISH,

ONE SOMETIMES WEARS PINK UNDERWEAR,

ONE FORCES ME TO BRUSH MY TEETH AND TAKE SHOWERS,

AND ONE OF THEM IS THE STRONGEST, SMARTEST, AND MOST HANDSOME BOY THAT EVER EXISTED.

FOR THE MOST PART,
MY LIFE IS TOTALLY RAD.

THE FIRST TIME MY PROBLEM ATTACKED ME
I WAS REALLY MAD BECAUSE MY DAD
(THE ONE THAT WEARS PINK UNDERWEAR)
WOULDN'T LET ME GO SWIMMING.

MY BRAIN SCRAMBLED LIKE EGGS

MY EYES SAW RED.

MY HEART FELT LIKE FIRE.

MY VOICE GOT DEEP.

MY TEETH GREW SHARP.

AND MY BUTT TOO TURNED
TO RED, STEAMING, HOT
LAVA!

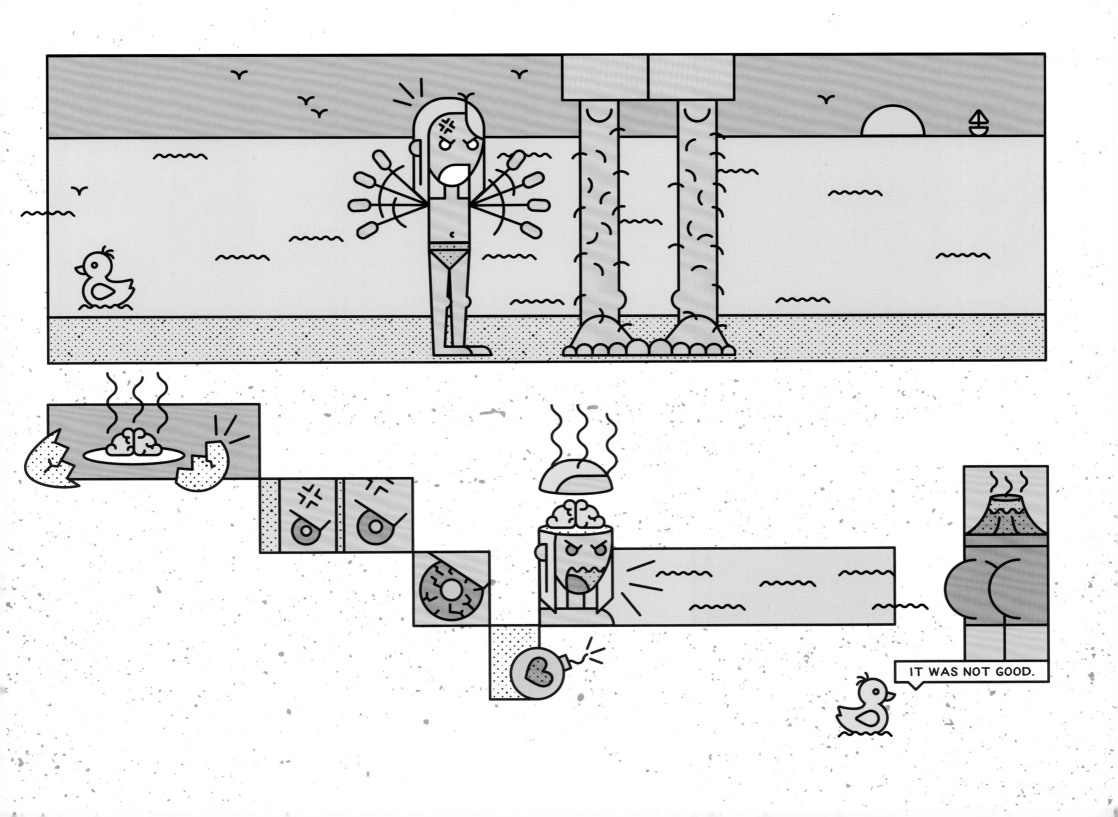

IT WAS NOT GOOD.

NOT ONLY WAS MY BUTT
TURNING TO RED-HOT
LAVA EVERY TIME I GOT
MAD, I STARTED TO
HURT OTHER PEOPLE
AND GETTING INTO
BIG-TIME TROUBLE.

ONCE I. WASN'T ALLOWED TO HAVE SPRITE AT DINNER

BECAUSE I PINCHED MY BROTHER (THE ONE WITH GREEN HAIR)

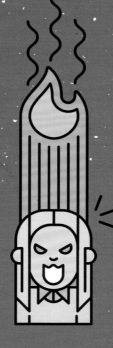

WHEN HE WOULDN'T MOVE HIS CHAIR.

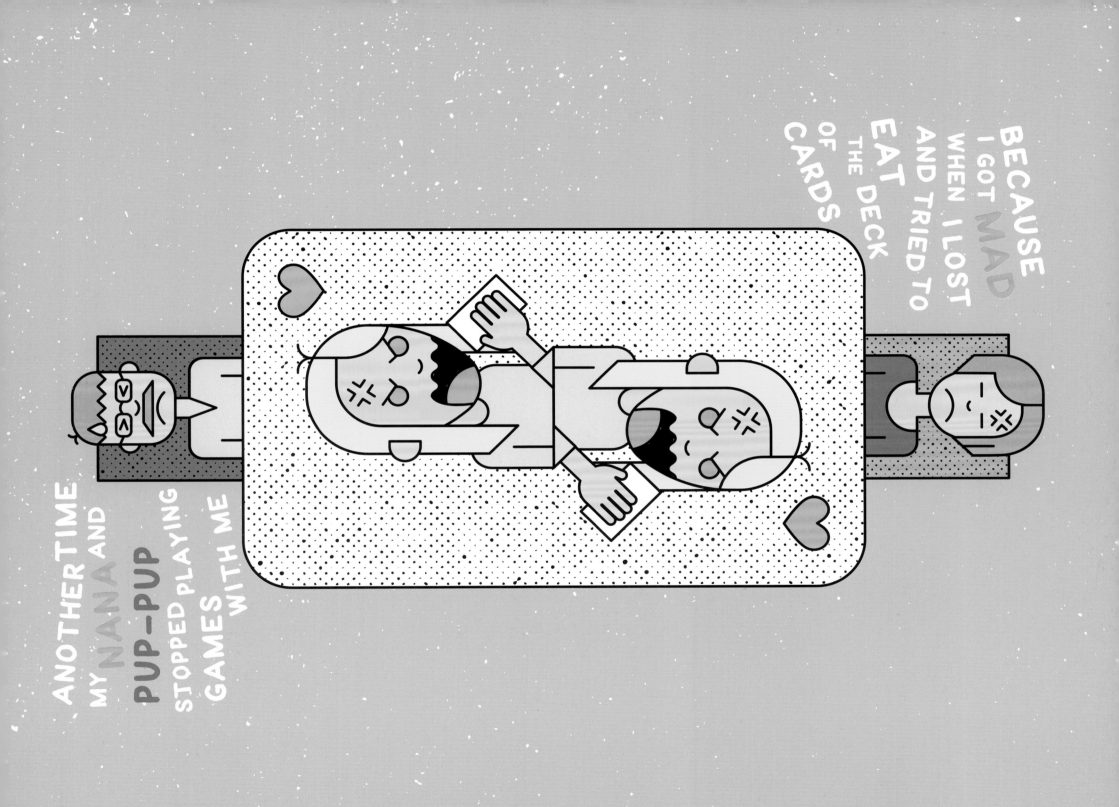

ANOTHER TIME
MY NANA AND
PUP-PUP
STOPPED PLAYING
GAMES WITH ME

BECAUSE
I GOT MAD
WHEN I LOST
AND TRIED TO
EAT
THE DECK
OF
CARDS

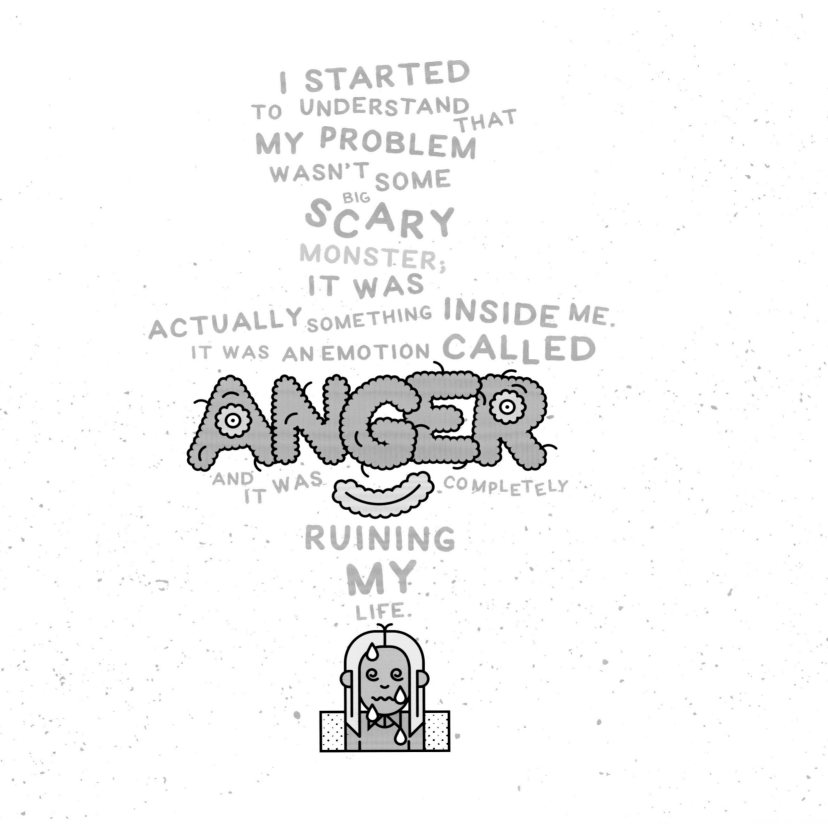

ONE SPRING, MY FAMILY WENT TO NEW YORK FOR VACATION. WE WERE SHOPPING FOR SOME BORING CLOTHES FOR MY MOM (THE ONE THAT POPS PIMPLES AND CUTS WARTS FOR WORK) WHEN I STARTED TO GET ANGRY...AGAIN.

BUT FOR SOME REASON, INSTEAD OF GETTING RED-HOT BOOTY MAD, I FOUND MYSELF SITTING NEXT TO A MANNEQUIN WITH MY LEGS CROSSED, HANDS IN THE AIR, CRISSED, AND EYES CLXSED.

MY BRAIN WAS FLOATING IN THE CLOUDS.

MY EYES SAW PEOPLE RUNNING AROUND IN THEIR UNDERWEAR.

MY BODY FELT LIKE IT WAS BEING TICKLED.

MY MOUTH TASTED PEACH, MOCHI ICE-CREAM

MY VOICE WAS ANGELIC.

MY TEETH WERE STRAIGHT, WHITE AND PERFECT (AGAIN).

MY BUTT FELT LIKE AN ICY COLD PUSH-POP ON A SUMMER DAY.

MY BABY SISTER (THE ONE THAT IS SASSY) SAW THAT SOMETHING WAS DIFFERENT, TAPPED ME ON THE SHOULDER AND ASKED WHAT I WAS DOING. WITHOUT MISSING A BEAT, I TOLD HER THAT I HAD GONE TO  UM LAND.

GO TO
UM LAND

WHEN YOU ARE LEARNING MULTIPLICATION FOR THE FIRST TIME AND IT'S HARD...

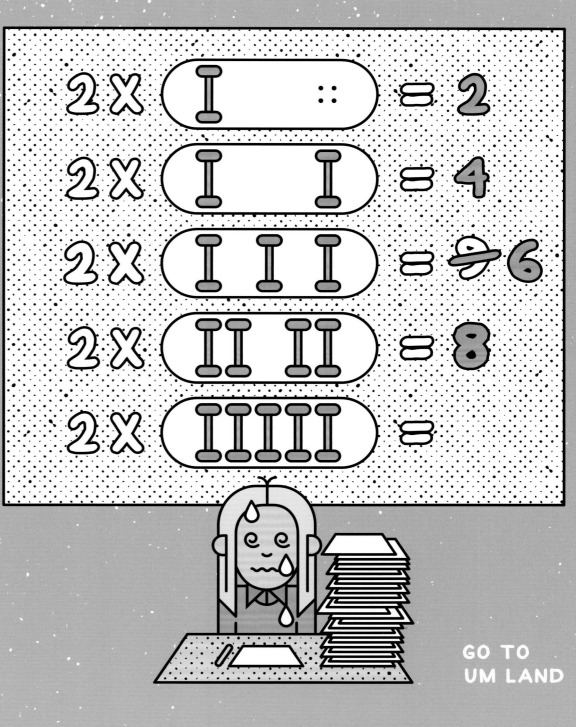

GO TO
UM LAND

WHEN YOU MISS A PARTY

BECAUSE YOU FELL ASLEEP...

GO TO
UM LAND

WHEN YOU'RE **SCARED** BECAUSE YOUR **DOG** IS HAVING A **SEIZURE...**

GO TO
UM LAND

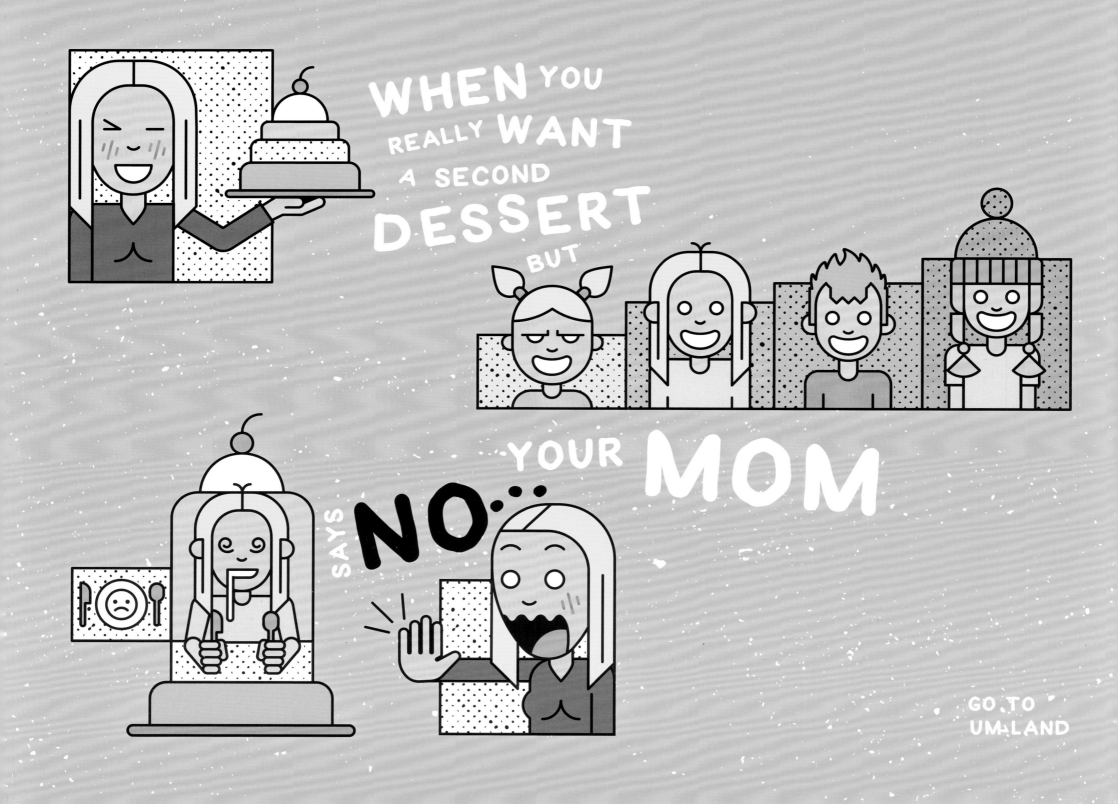

WHEN YOU
ARE FEELING NERVOUS
BEFORE A CHESS
TOURNAMENT

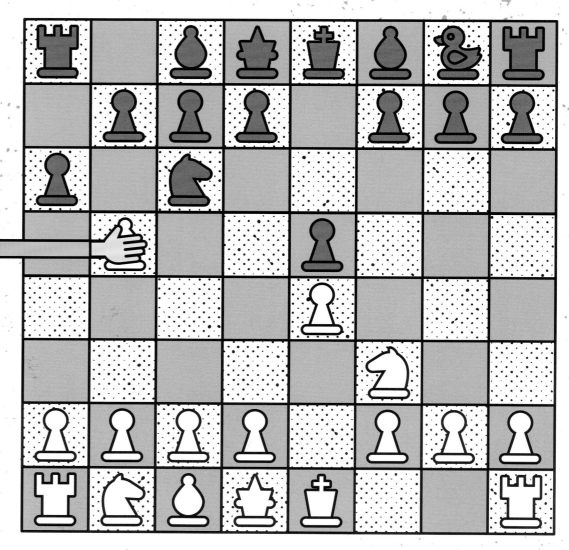

GO TO
UM LAND

WHEN YOUR **DAD** WON'T LET **YOU** SNUGGLE AT BEDTIME BECAUSE HE WANTS TO **GET** A **GOOD** NIGHTS SLEEP...

Z
Z
Z
z

GO TO
UM LAND

WHEN YOU ARE **BORED** SHOPPING FOR YOUR **MOM'S** CLOTHES IN **NEW YORK** CITY ...

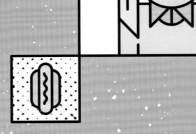

GO TO
UM LAND

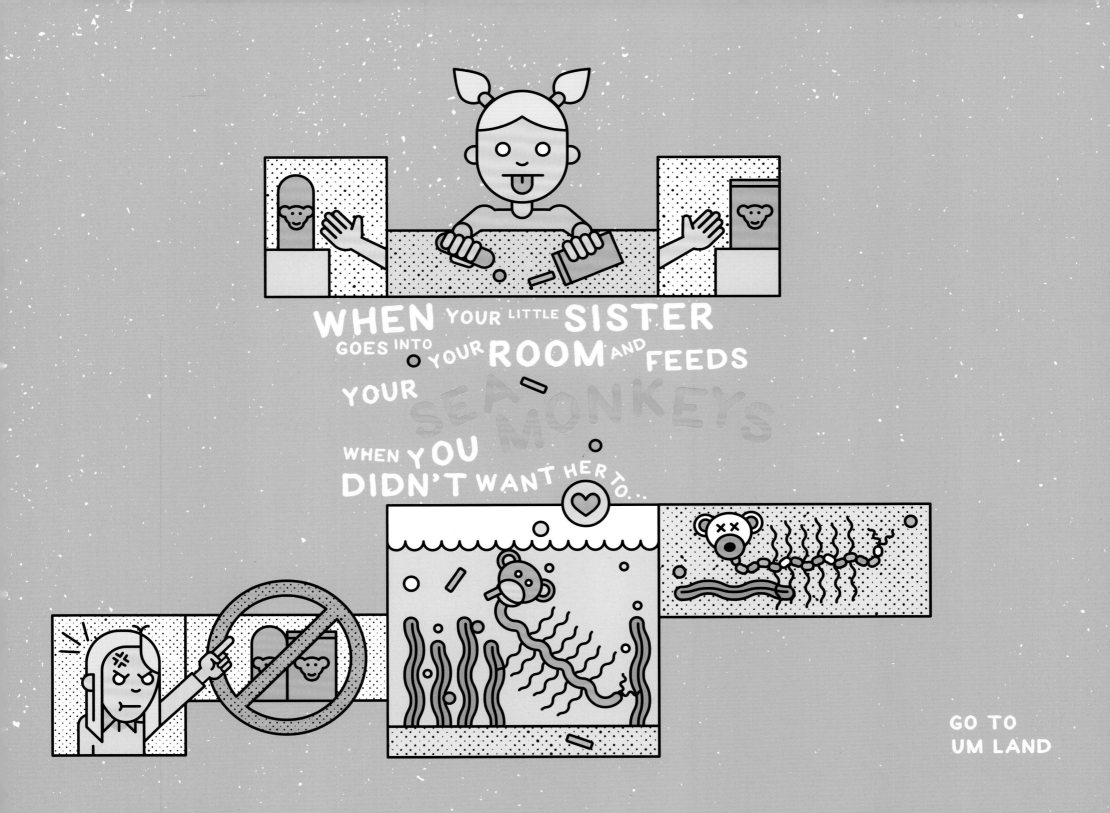

WHEN YOUR LITTLE SISTER GOES INTO YOUR ROOM AND FEEDS YOUR SEA MONKEYS WHEN YOU DIDN'T WANT HER TO...

GO TO
UM LAND

WHEN YOUR NANNY PUTS KETCHUP UNDER THE HOTDOG INSTEAD OF ON TOP...

GO TO
UM LAND

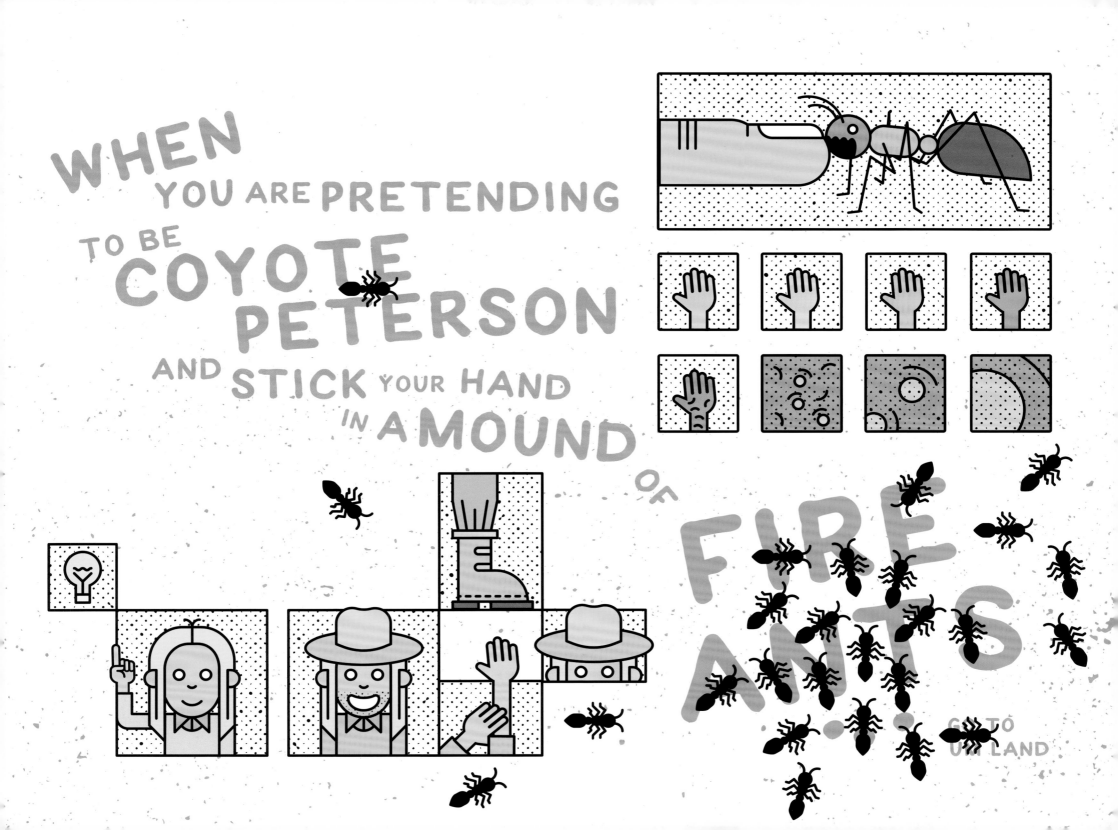

WHEN YOU ARE PRETENDING TO BE COYOTE PETERSON AND STICK YOUR HAND IN A MOUND OF FIRE ANTS...

WHEN YOUR **DAD** BUYS **YOU** A **POCKETKNIFE,**
BUT YOUR **MOM** WON'T LET YOU **HAVE IT**
BECAUSE SHE THINKS **YOU STABBED** YOURSELF

BUT **REALLY** YOU **JUST SPILLED**
A **TIGER BLOOD** FLAVORED ICY
ON YOUR **SHIRT...**

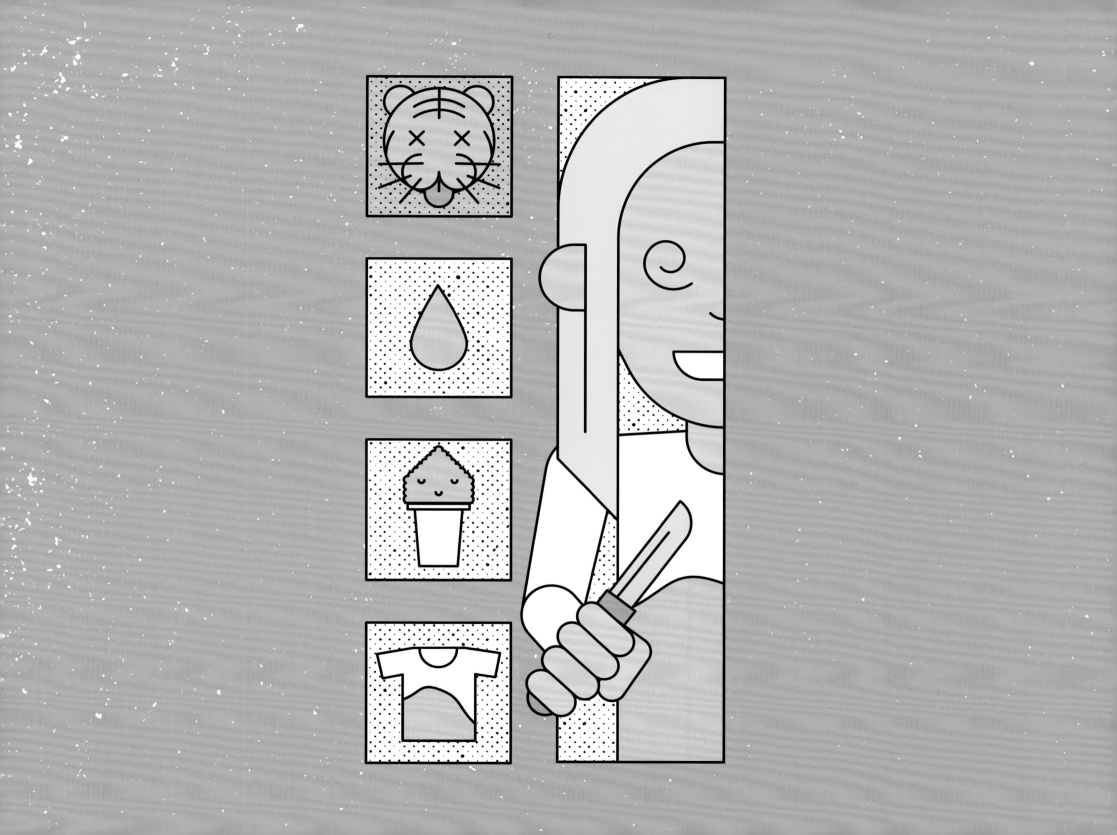

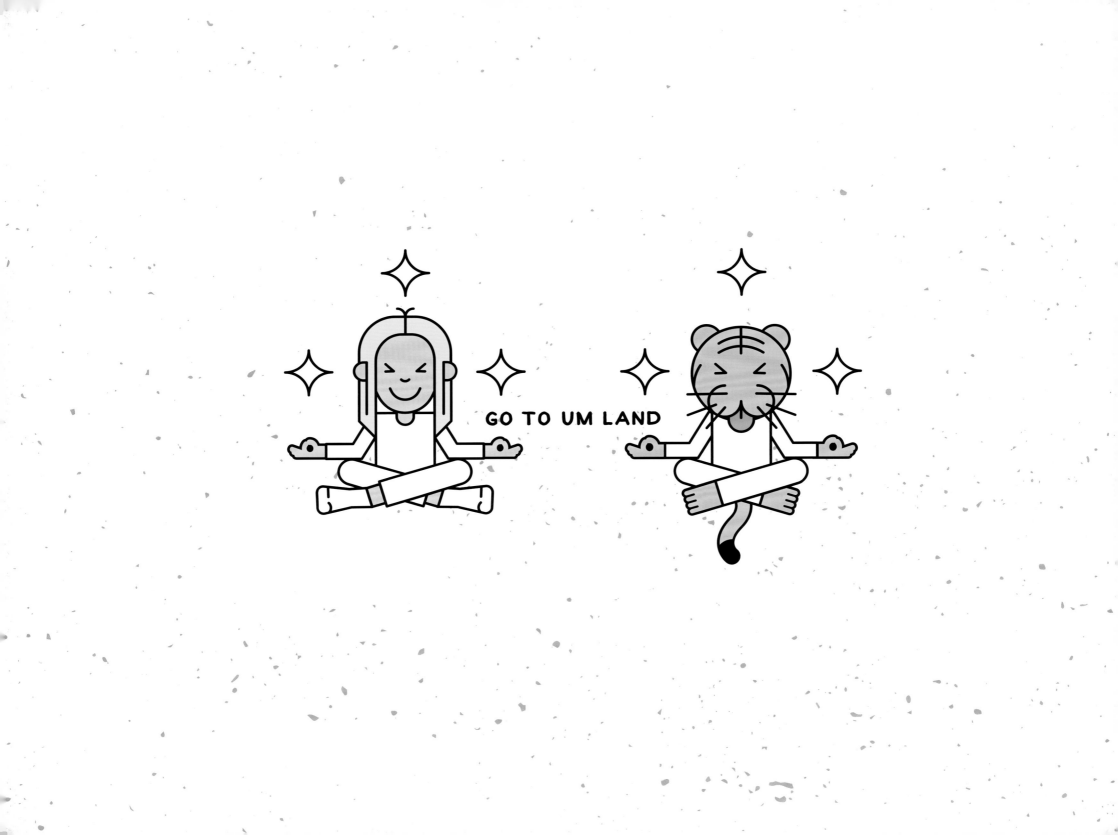

GO TO UM LAND

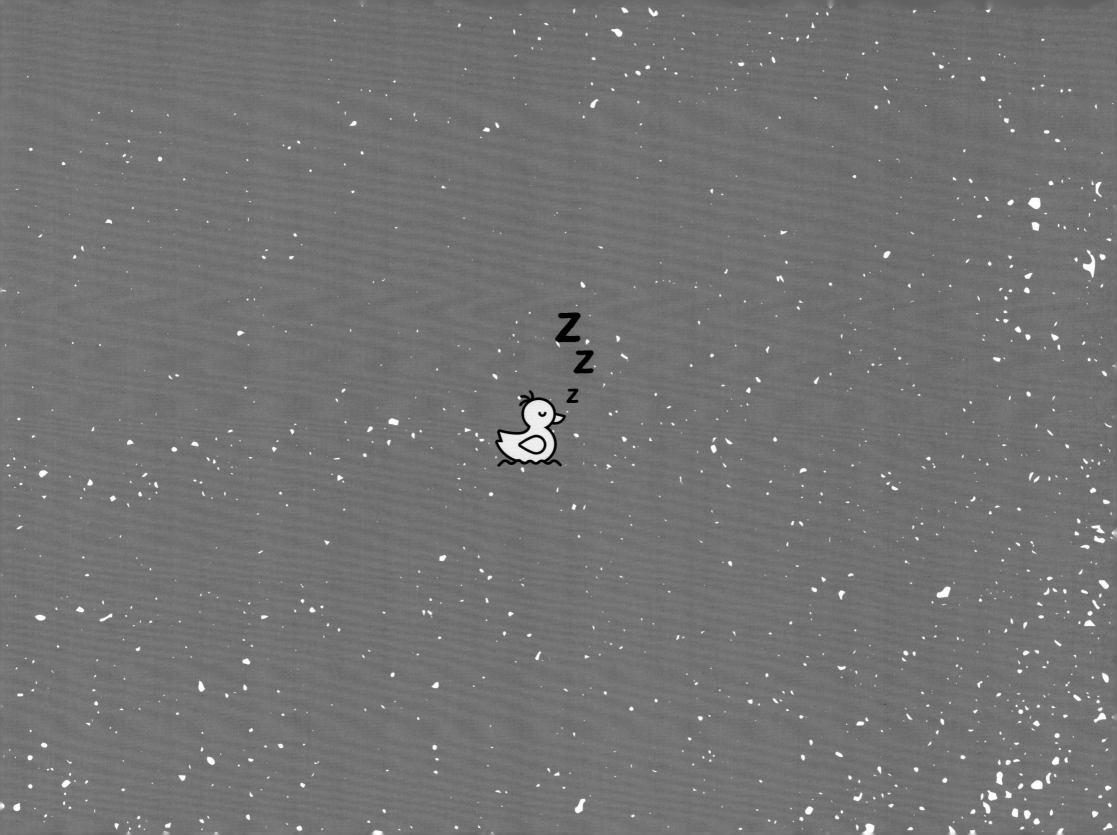

I WANTED TO TELL YOU ABOUT A BOOK I WROTE.
MY BOOK IS CALLED UM LAND. IT'S A BOOK IS FOR KIDS (WELL, REALLY ALL PEOPLE) TO LEARN WHAT TO DO WHEN THEY GET MAD, FRUSTRATED, SAD, OR FEEL ANY OTHER EMOTION THAT HURTS INSIDE.

I KNOW THAT PEOPLE WHO MEDITATE REALLY CALL IT "OHM", BUT I CALL IT "UM". MY MOM SAID THAT IS FINE BECAUSE I AM SIX, PLUS I REALLY LIKE UM BETTER.

I WANT TO TEACH EVERYONE HOW TO GO TO UM LAND BECAUSE IT IS AN AWESOME STATE OF MIND. GOING TO UM LAND IS REALLY EASY AND YOU CAN DO IT ANYTIME AND ANYWHERE. IT IS IN YOUR MIND AND HEART.

TO GO TO UM LAND JUST CRISSCROSS APPLESAUCE (THAT MEANS CROSS YOUR LEGS), CLOSE YOUR EYES, HANDS IN THE AIR, FINGERS TOGETHER, AND THINK FUNNY THOUGHTS. SOME FUNNY THOUGHTS THAT I LIKE ARE PEOPLE RUNNING AROUND IN THEIR UNDERWEAR, BEING TICKLED, AND PEOPLE DOING SILLY THINGS.

THE FIRST TIME I THOUGHT OF UM LAND WAS WHEN I WAS IN NEW YORK SHOPPING WITH MY MOM. I STARTED TO GET REALLY MAD, BUT INSTEAD OF SCREAMING, I DECIDED TO CLOSE MY EYES AND JUST RELAX. MY LITTLE SISTER ASKED WHAT I WAS DOING AND I TOLD HER I HAD GONE TO UM LAND. THAT IS HOW UM LAND WAS BORN!

ONCE I DISCOVERED UM LAND, I WROTE EVERY DAY ABOUT WHEN I COULD GO TO UM LAND. FOR EXAMPLE, **"WHEN YOU STICK YOUR HAND IN MOUND OF FIRE ANTS, GO TO UM LAND"**. OR "WHEN YOUR BROTHER PUSHES YOU OFF A TRAMPOLINE AND YOU NEED STITCHES, GO TO UM LAND".

AFTER A YEAR I HAD HUNDREDS OF UM LANDS WRITTEN. I HAD SO MANY I DECIDED TO PUT IT IN A BOOK. I BORROWED MY DAD'S OLD PHONE AND SAT OUTSIDE FOR A FEW DAYS AND RECORDED MY UM LAND STORY. IT INCLUDED A MONSTER, HOT LAVA BUTTS, AND MY FAVORITE TIMES TO GO TO UM LAND. THEN MY MOM AND DAD TOOK THE STORY FROM THE PHONE AND HELPED MY TYPE IT UP. YOU CAN FIND THE RECORDINGS ON MY WEBSITE, MYUMLAND.COM.

NEXT I NEEDED TO GET THE DRAWINGS MADE FOR MY BOOK. I ORGANIZED A CONTEST AND GAVE SEVEN DESIGNERS ONE-PAGE OF MY STORY. I GOT A LOT OF REALLY COOL ILLUSTRATIONS BACK, BUT THERE WAS ONE THAT WAS MY ABSOLUTE FAVORITE. **I WAS LAUGHING SO HARD I ALMOST PEED MY PANTS!**

I HOPE YOU LOVE MY UM LAND STORY AS MUCH AS I DO. I REALLY HOPE THAT PEOPLE DON'T JUST READ THE STORY, BUT START TO LIVE THE UM LAND LIFESTYLE. ANYTIME OR ANYWHERE, GO TO UM LAND TO MAKE YOURSELF FEEL BETTER.

WWW.MYUMLAND.COM

UM LAND IS GOOD.